William Ackland

How to Take Stereoscopic Pictures

Anatiposi

William Ackland

How to Take Stereoscopic Pictures

Reprint of the original.

1st Edition 2023 | ISBN: 978-3-38230-234-4

Anatiposi Verlag is an imprint of Outlook Verlagsgesellschaft mbH.

Verlag (Publisher): Outlook Verlag GmbH, Zeilweg 44, 60439 Frankfurt, Deutschland
Vertretungsberechtigt (Authorized to represent): E. Roepke, Zeilweg 44, 60439 Frankfurt, Deutschland
Druck (Print): Books on Demand GmbH, In de Tarpen 42, 22848 Norderstedt, Deutschland

HOW TO TAKE

STEREOSCOPIC PICTURES,

INCLUDING A

Detailed Account of the Necessary Apparatus,

AND A MINUTE DESCRIPTION OF

THE COLLODIO-ALBUMEN, FOTHERGILL'S,

AND

POWELL'S DRY PROCESS.

By WILLIAM ACKLAND.

THIRD EDITION.

SIMPKIN, MARSHALL, & CO., STATIONER'S HALL COURT;

AND

HORNE & THORNTHWAITE,

Opticians and Photographic Instrument Makers,

BY SPECIAL APPOINTMENT

TO HER MAJESTY,

Nos. 121, 122, 123, NEWGATE STREET, LONDON, E.C.

1859.

HOW TO TAKE

STEREOSCOPIC PICTURES.

ON BINOCULAR VISION AND THE STEREOSCOPE.

THE study of Binocular Vision is one of the most fascinating branches of Optics, and has long afforded ample scope for the theorist; but the practical application of its principles is only of recent date. It is a fact but little known, though indisputable, that if a solid object is viewed with both eyes, or with each eye in succession, the image of that object formed on one retina is quite different from that which is formed upon the other; yet these two dissimilar pictures, united, give to the mind the impression of a solid, having rotundity, depth, and thickness.

Now, as we find that such a result is caused by the impression of the two different pictures on the retina, we are led to inquire what would be the effect of reversing the process; so that, instead of viewing one solid object, and impressing the retinæ with two dissimilar pictures, we viewed two dissimilar pictures of the same object, and united, by squinting, the images formed on the retinæ. This experiment has been made, and it is proved that the combined pictures will give the appearance of a solid in relief, having all the usual characteristic of one,—namely, rotundity, depth, and thickness.

The two dissimilar pictures of the same object may be united

B

with much greater facility by being viewed in the Stereoscope, as this instrument renders the illusion more perfect.

The original Stereoscope, as first introduced by Professor Wheatstone, consists of two parallel Mirrors placed with their edges in contact, and inclined at right angles one to the other. These Mirrors are attached to a vertical support which slides into the centre of a Base-board, about three feet long. Near the two ends of this Base-board are supports for receiving the pictures, which are so placed that they shall face each other. On looking into the two Mirrors at the same time, the images of the two pictures are formed on the same portion of each retina, conveying to the mind an impression of an object in relief.

This form of Stereoscope is adapted for viewing large pictures, but is not so successful when applied to small ones of two or three inches square.

For viewing small stereoscopic pictures, the Refracting Stereoscope, invented by Sir David Brewster, is more useful. This deservedly popular instrument, now so generally known, consists of a pyramidal body of wood about $5\frac{1}{2}$ inches high, surmounted at the top by two Eye-pieces, separated from each other a distance equal to the space between the two eyes (about $2\frac{5}{8}$ inches). Each of these Eye-pieces contains the half of a Lens, about 6 inches focus. The body of the Stereoscope is pierced near the base to form a receptacle for the picture to be viewed; and a small door in front, when opened, admits the passage of light to illuminate opaque pictures.

If we take two correct drawings of any object from two different points of view, and place them in the Stereoscope, we shall find, on looking through the instrument, that the two plane representations inserted within will appear united, forming one solid representation of the most perfect description. But this truly wonderful result cannot be obtained, unless the drawings are exact copies of nature, more exact than the human hand can execute; therefore we call another science to our aid, and have recourse to sun-pictures.

Photography enables us to obtain with great facility the most truthful pictures, correct in every detail and perfect in every shade, whether portraits, groups, studies, or views; and these are rendered more life-like when viewed in relief by the aid of the Stereoscope, thus making the illusion so complete as to astonish the beholder.

To describe plainly and practically the mode of producing such representations by Photography has been my aim in this treatise. If the reader finds from my directions as much gratification as I have obtained whilst preparing them, I shall be fully rewarded.

In order to produce pictures by Photography, certain apparatus is indispensable; but I propose describing only what is needed to produce pictures suitable for being viewed by the Refracting Stereoscope; my reasons for this limitation being:—

1st.—That double pictures seen in the Stereoscope convey to an observer a more pleasing and correct impression than could possibly be derived from viewing a single picture, although treble the size.

2nd.—The bulk of the apparatus necessary for stereoscopic pictures is more easy of transport than that for taking single pictures of a moderately large size. Indeed, all that is required for taking eight stereoscopic views may be carried without much inconvenience for miles, as the weight does not exceed six pounds; whereas the weight of the necessary apparatus to take single views of even seven inches by six would be at least three times more.

The apparatus necessary for taking stereoscopic pictures consists of

1. Camera.
2. Lens.
3. Camera Stand and Screw.
4. Focussing Eye-piece.
5. View Meter.
6. Focussing Cloth.
7. Spirit Level.

Fig 1.

THE STEREOSCOPIC CAMERA.

A Camera adapted for taking stereoscopic pictures is represented by Fig. 1, the body of which is of the form commonly
used for taking portraits; but the receptacle *a*, to receive the

Fig 2.

Camera-back (Fig. 2), is placed horizontally when in use. The
Camera is fixed on the cross-bar *c* of the Base-board (Fig. 3).
This cross-bar connects two parallel bars *b b*, which are capable
of adjustment by the right and left handed screw *e e*. The
Camera-back (Fig. 2) serves to receive the Sensitized Plate, and

protects it from light. It consists of a frame of wood, with projecting slips on its two longest edges, which fit into the

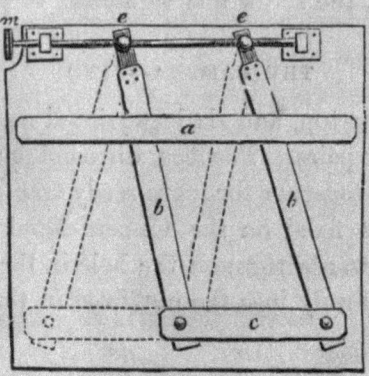

Fig. 3.

channels of the receptacle *a* (Fig. 1). On either side of this frame is a flap, the one hinged and the other sliding; and within, a frame with silver wire corners. The Sensitive Plate is placed in this Camera-back by raising the hinged flap, and allowing the plate to drop in, so that *the sensitive surface rests on the silver wires.* The hinged flap is then closed, and the brass buttons turned, to prevent it again opening. If we intend conveying it to a distance before exposing it in the Camera it is advisable to secure the sliding flap from being accidentally opened, by passing a vulcanised band around the Camera-back. This band must, of necessity, be removed when the back is placed in the Camera; but it is a wise precaution to replace it as soon as possible, for the slightest gleam of light falling on the Plate, either before or after exposure, would inevitably spoil the result.

The Focussing Screen fits into the receptacle *a*, and consists of a frame of wood containing a plate of glass very finely ground. Its use is to ascertain when a proper focus is obtained. This Screen should have a vertical pencil line ruled on it to serve as a guide in adjusting the bars *b b* (Fig. 3). The Camera admits of being expanded on the screw *e* being loosened, in order to get an approximate focus, and the finer adjustment is obtained by turning the milled head of the Lens. When the proper focus is obtained, the screw *e* is tightened to prevent shifting.

THE CAMERA-STAND

Consists of a brass top, and six legs jointed near to the bottom so as to form three pairs. The legs, when not in use, fold closely, and are strapped together for more ready transport.

The Camera is fixed on the Camera-stand by passing the Fixing Screw upwards through the hole in the Stand-top, and then screwing it firmly into the nut fixed in the centre of the Base-board.

STEREOSCOPIC LENS.

In order to take stereoscopic views effectually, a Single Achromatic Lens must be employed. A short focus Portrait Lens even when used with a small diaphragm, will not produce such good results; and after trying a number of experiments with a great variety of Lenses of different foci, I am led to form the opinion that Horne and Thornthwaite's Stereoscopic Lenses stand unrivalled for taking views;* and if stereoscopic portraits are needed, a portrait combination may be so fitted into it as to screw into the same flange, and thus a change of Lenses may be easily made. The tourist will find this arrangement very useful; for, after taking various scenes with the single Lens, he may encounter the rustic peasantry of the country, and wish to fix their lineaments on the Plate, which he could not accomplish by any other means. The time of sitting required by the single Achromatic Lens would be too long and tedious; and here the double, or portrait combination, would be found useful.

* Horne and Thornthwaite have lately introduced a *Large-angle* Stereo-scopic Lens of 3¾ inch focus, which is peculiarly adapted for taking views of buildings, &c., in very confined situations, as by its aid the Camera may be placed much nearer the object than could be possible with a Lens of longer focus.

It will be found extremely convenient to have two Single Achromatic Lenses of different foci screwing into the same brass mounting; one of 4¼ inch focus for taking buildings, groups of trees, &c., where no long distance intervenes; and another of 5¼ inches for taking buildings, &c., with distance, or in taking panoramas of a country from elevated situations.

The first named Lens will be found the most generally useful, but distant objects taken by it are too minute; and in order to render these of a more visible size, the longer focus lens is to be selected.

Fig. 4.

FOCUSSING EYE-PIECE.

This little instrument (Fig. 4) is used in order to assist the sight in focussing, as described in the section on that subject.

Fig. 5.

THE VIEW-METER.

This useful appendage to the photographic outfit consists of a conical-shaped box, open at either end, as represented by Fig. 5. If held by the ring, so that the smaller end is near the eye, on looking through it the larger end will expose just as much of the view as the Camera, fitted with the 4¼ inch focus Lens, will take in, if placed in the same situation.

The exact position where to "set-up" the Camera is easily determined, and the selection of the best point of view readily made by its aid. For this important reason, the little instrument should always occupy a place in the amateur's pocket when on a ramble, as, although he may not be then out for photographic purposes, he may wish to ascertain the fitness of a particular point of view at which, on some future time, to plant his Camera, or to ascertain whether or not the view before him is suitable, and how much could be taken in by his Camera.

It may be noticed that the View-meter is required to be constructed to suit the focal length of the lens employed, and of the picture produced; consequently, a View-meter constructed for one lens will not answer for another of a different focal length.

FOCUSSING CLOTH.

A Focussing Cloth is absolutely essential, and is best constructed of a black waterproof material. Its use is described in the section on Focussing.

Fig. 6.

CIRCULAR SPIRIT-LEVEL.

It is a point of some importance, when taking views, that the Camera should be perfectly level. This is easily effected by placing a circular Spirit-level on the Camera, and moving the Camera-stand legs, until the spirit-bubble is exactly in the centre of the level.*

* However carefully this level is constructed, it sometimes happens that evaporation of the spirit takes place, and the bubble becomes too large. To remedy this, remove the screw, add a sufficiency of Alcohol to reduce the bubble to the size of a small pea, and replace the screw as before.

PORTABLE STEREOSCOPIC CAMERA.

Registered, December 27, 1858, by John Harrison Powell.

Fig. 7.

This form of Camera (Fig. 7) is an improvement on the foregoing, and is the lightest, most portable, and easiest of manipulation, of any yet invented.

The drawing below (Fig. 8) exhibits the apparatus when closed, in which condition it is carried by the leather handle on the top. It contains all that is necessary for taking eight stereoscopic pictures by any of the dry processes. The outside measurement is $9 \times 5\frac{1}{2} \times 6$ inches, and the weight is five pounds.

Full directions for using this Camera will be found at page 39.

Fig. 8.   Fig. 9.

In addition to the foregoing, which would be required for out-door use, the articles which follow as far as the foot of p. 12, are needed for use at home, to prepare the Plates, for developing, fixing, exciting, &c.

DIPPING-BATH.

The Dipping-bath is employed for exciting the Plates in the Bath Solution, and may be either horizontal or vertical. The horizontal Bath consists of a glass tray, with upright sides, and is usually a trifle larger inside than the Plate to be excited. A silver hook is to be used with this and the "Well-bath," in order to lower and raise the Plate in and out of the solution.

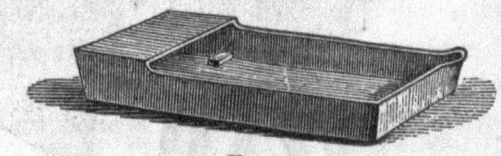

Fig. 10.

The "Well-bath" is another form of Dipping-bath, and is the most convenient for rendering the Plate sensitive during travelling, as it requires a very small quantity of Bath Solution to excite a Plate.

The vertical Dipping-bath is used to excite the Collodion film, and is represented by Fig. 9; the Bath is generally made of glass or gutta-percha, and the Dipper of glass.

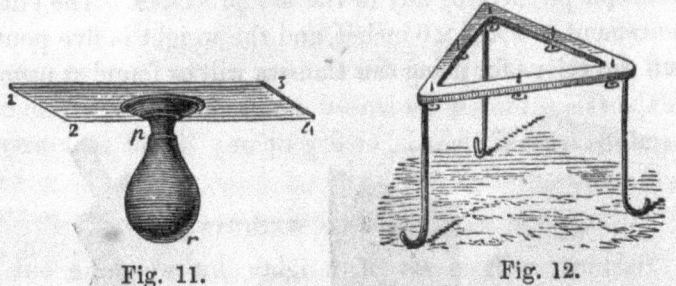

Fig. 11.   Fig. 12.

GLOBE PLATE-HOLDER.

The most convenient form of Plate-holder is represented by Fig. 11. It is fixed to, and serves as a handle for, the Plate during the coating.

LEVELLING STAND.

For the purpose of keeping the Glass Plate perfectly level during washing and developing, a Levelling Stand is employed, such as Fig. 12. In order to set it level, a glass plate, supporting a Circular Level, Fig. 6, is placed on the top, so as to rest on the screws; and one or more of the screws is raised or depressed, until the spirit-bubble is exactly in the centre—thus indicating that the Glass Plate is perfectly horizontal.

GLASS ROD.

A Glass Rod is very useful to stir up any substance resting at the bottom of a liquid in which it is to be dissolved, and for mixing together two or more solutions, to ensure a perfect admixture. Very great care must be used to keep it perfectly clean, or solutions stirred with it may become contaminated and useless.

GRADUATED GLASS MEASURE.

For the purpose of measuring quantities of solution, a two-ounce Graduated Measure is required. This is divided on one side into sixteen drams, and the other into two ounces. In using it, hold it up level with the eye, and pour in the liquid until it rises to the mark indicating the required quantity. A measure holding half-a-pint is also useful.

CLOTHS.

Two carefully-washed cloths of "fine diaper" are required to clean the Glass Plates, Measures, &c., and a third, of common material, to wipe the hands, or dry up any liquid that may be spilt.

BALANCE AND WEIGHTS.

A Balance, with a set of weights, for weighing out the quantities of chemicals, is necessary. The pans should be of glass, and must be kept perfectly clean. The large weights, up to two drams, are stamped with their respective weights, and the smaller ones have figures or dots representing grains.

FUNNELS.

Two Funnels will be found useful—a small one of glass, and a larger one of gutta-percha. The latter should be so made that the small one will fit inside it, thus economising space, and preventing fracture during travelling.

FILTERING PAPER.

This can be obtained either ready cut into circles to fit the Funnel, or in quires. Two sizes of circular Filters will be needed, and about half a quire of filtering paper.

DEVELOPING GLASSES.

A set of three Developing Glasses, the largest of which contains about two ounces, will be found very useful.

Fig. 13.

PRESSURE FRAME.

For the purpose of reproducing transparent Positive pictures from glass Negatives, a Pressure Frame of the form of Fig. 13 will be required.

Fig. 14.

WASHING TRAYS.

Two descriptions of Washing Trays are required; one shallow, and about half an inch each way larger than the Plate, for washing after the Collodion Bath in Fothergill's process; and a deep Washing Tray, Fig. 14, for washing off the Albumen in Fothergill's process, or for washing both films in the Collodio-albumen process.

Having given a description of the apparatus necessary for taking stereoscopic pictures, the next step will be to determine what process we shall adopt in order to ensure success in our photographic attempts: and in order that the reader may have a choice of dry processes, I have deemed it prudent to publish three—viz., the Collodio-albumen, Fothergill's, and Powell's dry process.

The Collodio-albumen process produces pictures possessing fine middle tint, considerable softness, and depths of shade; but the manipulations are complex. The Negatives, from their peculiar colour, print slowly, and the Sensitive Plates are deficient in keeping qualities.

Fothergill's process yields results of great beauty and softness: the manipulations are few and easy; the Negatives print with more readiness than Collodio-albumen Negatives; and the Excited Plates have been kept with impunity for months.

Powell's new dry process has now been in use some months, and appears to possess all the advantages of both the foregoing without their disadvantages. The Negatives are clear and soft, with abundance of middle tint: the skies are dense; the deep shades well brought out; the contrast of light and shade artistically marked: whilst, in my hands, its power of rendering imperfectly illuminated foreground and distance is unequalled by *any* process.

COLLODIO-ALBUMEN PROCESS.

In describing this process I propose to make free use of the excellent remarks and formula of Mr. Joseph Sidebottom, of Manchester, whose productions by this process have been pronounced, by competent authority, to "possess all the softness and beautiful gradation of half-tone, which we are accustomed to look upon as the distinguishing characteristic of the Wet Collodion process."

Before entering into a description of the manipulation, an enumeration of the necessary Solutions, and directions for preparing such as are not purchased ready made, will be needed. These solutions are—

Plate Cleaning Solution.
Tincture of Iodine.
Iodized Collodion.
Iodized Albumen.
Bath Solution.
Aceto-nitrate Bath Solution.
Pyrogallic Acid Solution.
Silver Developing Solution.
Fixing Solution.

PLATE CLEANING SOLUTION.

This solution is supplied by Horne and Thornthwaite, mixed ready for use in four ounce bottles, at sixpence each.

TINCTURE OF IODINE.

Iodine - - - - - - - 1 dram.
Alcohol - - - - - 1 ounce.

Mix.

IODIZED COLLODION.*

The Collodion necessary for this purpose must be such as, when poured on a plate of glass, yields a transparent and slightly coherent film, which does not admit of being lifted

---

* It will not escape the notice of the reader that Powell's Collodion is recommended for the three dry processes described in this work. This recommendation is the result of careful experiments long continued, and offers the amateur an opportunity of testing either process without the trouble of obtaining (perhaps at a distance) Collodions specially suited to each process, as was formerly the case.

The Tincture of Iodine added to it, appears quickly to render the film it produces sufficiently porous for use in the Collodio-albumen process; but this addition is not to be employed where the Collodion is intended for either Fothergill's or Powell's process.

entire from the glass, and has a roughened surface when viewed microscopically. These properties are not possessed by ordinary Collodion recently iodized; but Powell's Collodion, after being iodized as described below, will answer the purpose. It is much improved for use in this process after being iodized a week, and may be used even after being iodized for months.

In order to iodize this Collodion for use, add two drams of Powell's Iodizing Solution, and ten drops of Tincture of Iodine, to six drams of his Collodion; shake well together, and then allow the bottle to remain undisturbed for at least one hour, in order that any insoluble particles may settle to the bottom; then pour off into a clean and perfectly dry bottle for use.

In operating with this volatile article, never approach with a light near the open bottle, or accidents may arise from its inflammable character.

IODIZED ALBUMEN.

Albumen (white of egg) - - -	3 ounces.
Distilled or Filtered Rain Water -	¾ ounce.
Liquor Ammonia - - - -	½ dram.
Iodide of Potassium - - -	15 grains.
Bromide of Potassium - - -	3 grains.
Tincture of Iodine - - -	1 drop.

Dissolve the Iodide and Bromide of Potassium in the water; then add the Liquor Ammonia and Tincture of Iodine, and stir well together with a glass rod; then put this mixture and the Albumen into a basin capable of holding a quart : beat up for twenty minutes, into a complete froth, with a silver fork (not a steel one) or a bundle of half a dozen quills; allow it to remain all night undisturbed; then filter through a piece of fine sponge, plugged into the neck of a clear glass funnel; and stow away, in two ounce well-corked bottles, for use. A small fragment of Camphor put in each bottle will preserve this Iodized Albumen for many months, more especially if kept in a cool place.

BATH SOLUTION.

Nitrate of Silver, fused   -   -   1 ounce.*
Iodide of Potassium   -   -   -   2 grains.
Glacial Acetic Acid   -   -   -   4 drops.
Alcohol   -   -   -   -   -   1 dram.
Ether   -   -   -   -   -   -   1 dram.
Distilled or Filtered Rain Water -   12 ounces.

Dissolve the Nitrate of Silver in three ounces of the water, and the Iodide of Potassium in one ounce of water. Mix these two solutions, shake well, then add the remaining eight ounces of water, and filter to separate the yellow precipitate which is formed, and to the filtered liquid add the Acetic Acid, Alcohol, and Ether.

This solution will remain in perfect action sometimes for months, merely requiring the addition of a little fused Nitrate of Silver to be added from time to time, to keep up the solution to its original strength.

ACETO-NITRATE BATH SOLUTION.

Nitrate of Silver, fused -   -   -   1½ ounce.*
Glacial Acetic Acid   -   -   -   1 ounce.
Distilled Water   -   -   -   -   16 ounces.

Dissolve the Nitrate of Silver in the distilled water; then add the Acetic acid and filter for use.

This solution soon becomes discoloured by use. In order to render it colourless and preserve it in that state, keep it, when not in use, in a bottle containing about a quarter of an ounce of Kaolin; but it must be most carefully filtered, so as to separate this substance before being used.

---

* Nitrate of Silver and other chemicals were sold by the Avoirdupois ounce of 437½ grains; and it is this and not the Troy ounce of 480 grains, that is here to be employed.

PYROGALLIC SOLUTION.

Pyrogallic Acid - - - - 6 grains.
Glacial Acetic Acid - - - 1 dram.
Distilled or Filtered Rain Water - 3 ounces.

Dissolve and Filter.

This solution will not keep good more than a few days in summer.

SILVER DEVELOPING SOLUTION.

Nitrate of Silver - - - - 10 grains.
Distilled or Filtered Rain Water - 5 ounces.

Dissolve.

FIXING SOLUTION.

Hyposulphite of Soda - - - 4 ounces.
Water - - - - - 16 ounces.

Dissolve.

For the benefit of the non-chemical reader, we will point out the keeping qualities of these solutions:—

The Cleansing Mixture, Tincture of Iodine, Iodized Collodion, Silver Developing Solution, and Fixing Solution, will keep good any length of time.

The Pyrogallic Acid Solution cannot be depended on if they have been made longer than four days.

The Bath and Aceto-nitrate Solutions do not change by keeping, but require the addition of Nitrate of Silver, after being used to excite about forty Plates; and if it becomes brown, the addition of a little more Kaolin will remedy the defect.

The quantity of Nitrate of Silver to be added to restore these solutions to their original strength will be found by using the Bath-tester as described at page 48 in this work.

c

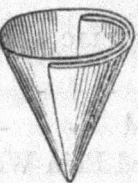

Fig. 14.

FILTRATION.

Filtering is an operation that requires to be done at almost every step in photographic manipulation, in order to separate any floating or insoluble particles from solutions, and is performed as follows:—A circular piece of Filtering Paper is folded in half twice, so as to form, when opened, a paper cone, as shown in Fig. 14; this is placed within a glass or porcelain funnel, and a bottle or other glass vessel is placed underneath the funnel to receive the filtered liquid. The solution to be filtered is poured in a gentle stream against the double side of the paper cone until the fluid rises to within a quarter of an inch of the upper edge. Immediately the paper cone becomes wetted, the liquid will percolate through, and drop into the vessel placed to receive it, becoming in most cases perfectly clear: but if such is not the case, allow the filtration to proceed for a few minutes; then return what has passed through the funnel to be again filtered a second time, or until it is quite free from any floating particles. As Iodized Albumen filters very slowly through, and soon clogs up the pores of Filtering Paper, a fragment of sponge, pressed lightly into the neck of a funnel, must be employed instead.

THE OPERATING ROOM.

In order to prepare our Sensitive Plates, and properly to develop the picture, an operating room is absolutely necessary. By this it is not meant that a room built expressly is needed; for almost any room can, in a few minutes, be made to serve our required wants: but the only absolute condition that must not be deviated from is that no light shall enter the room except what passes through three thicknesses of yellow glazed calico. The most convenient room is one facing the north, and with one window only. Prevent any light passing in by the upper half of the window, by closing the shutters or covering it with any black material impervious to light, and cover the lower half with three thicknesses of yellow calico. Close the door, and carefully observe if any gleam of light enters the room, except what passes through the yellow calico; should any crevice be detected, it must be covered over, as the intrusion of white light through the smallest chink is often sufficient to spoil a picture, although light that passes through three thicknesses of yellow calico does not affect the picture, and affords sufficient illumination for all our operations.

A table placed close to the window, a gutta-percha tray to receive any liquid that may fall in developing, a good supply of cold water, a hand-basin, and a couple of linen cloths, complete all the requirements.

It will sometimes happen in travelling that a room may fall to our lot which would give us too much trouble to convert into one fit for the purpose. In that case our manipulation must be performed under a Photographic Tent, or deferred until night, and an ordinary candle placed behind a double thickness of yellow calico may be our source of light.

CLEANING THE PLATE.

It is advisable to use none but the best patent Plate-glass, and the edges should be just sufficiently ground to prevent the sharp corners cutting the fingers. This is easily effected by using an article made expressly for the purpose, and sold under the title of " Corundum Files."

To clean a new Glass Plate, pour four or five drops of the Plate-cleaning solution over the centre of the Plate, and with a pledget of linen well rub it over every part of back and front ; then, without waiting for the Plate to dry, remove all traces of

moisture with a linen cloth, and polish with another linen
cloth, holding the Plate by the cloth and not by the hand, so
as to prevent the slightest grease being communicated to it.
The cloths employed should be of a material sold as "fine
diaper," and must be well freed from grease or soap, by careful
washing in soda and water, then plentifully rinsed in water
and dried; also the one used as a polisher should be kept
quite dry. Occasional breathing on the Plate during the
polishing, and then holding it obliquely, so that the moisture
deposited may be seen by reflected light, will serve to point
out whether a Plate is clean or not. If the moisture of the
breath is deposited in patches, more cleaning is required; but
if the deposit is evenly spread over the whole surface, it may
safely be considered as clean. Glass Plates, after being once
used, require to soak an hour in a solution of four ounces of
common washing soda to one pint of water, so that the har-
dened coating may be softened and easily rubbed off: they
have then to be cleaned as before mentioned for new Plates.

COATING WITH IODIZED COLLODION.

Before proceeding to coat the Plate, it is necessary that the
Iodized Collodion should have been allowed to stand for an
hour or more, so that any floating particles may fall to the
bottom; and in all cases the dust and dried crust of the
Collodion which may adhere to the neck of the bottle must
be carefully removed, otherwise spots or stains will be produced
on the Plate.

If particles of dust are floating in the air of the operating
room, it will be useless to attempt to coat a Plate, as they will
deposit themselves on it and serve as a nucleus for a stain in the
after-process. For this reason it is recommended to clean the
Plates in another room, so as not to disturb the atmosphere of
the operating room from this cause.

Having ascertained that the Glass Plate is perfectly clean,
and DRY, grasp it firmly by applying the tips of the fingers

and thumb of the left hand to the longest edge, then take the neck *p* of the Plate-holder (Fig. 11) between the first and second finger of the right hand; press the ball at *r* inwards with the thumb, and apply the concave part to the centre of the Glass Plate; remove the pressure of the thumb, and the Plate will be found to adhere.*

When such is the case, transfer the ball to the left hand, and hold it so that the Glass Plate shall be horizontal; then remove the stopper from the Iodized Collodion bottle, and, holding it in the right hand, pour the Collodion on the Glass Plate in snfficient quantity to form a circular pool extending to near the edges; next incline the Plate so that the fluid may flow to corner No. 4, Fig. 11, then to No. 3, then to No. 2, and drain the superfluous Collodion back into the bottle by corner No. 1, holding the Plate in a vertical direction. Give the Plate a rocking motion on the neck of the bottle by very lightly raising and depressing corner No. 4, so that any lines or furrows which are formed may run into each other. Continue this until the covered surface of the Plate appears *well* set from the evaporation of the Ether; when this takes place, compress the ball of the Plate-holder and detach it from the Plate. Now lay the Plate Collodion-side upwards on a glass Dipper, and plunge it with *one downward movement* in the Vertical bath (Fig. 9) filled to within an inch of the top with the Bath Solution, made as described at page 16, and carefully filtered. After the Plate has been allowed to remain in the Bath one minute, it is lifted out two or three times, in order to facilitate the removal of the *oily appearance* which the Plate now presents. When the surface appears uniformly wetted, the Plate is removed from the Dipper, and the excess of solution drained off; it is then placed, Collodion-side upwards, in a Washing Tray, Fig. 14, filled with clear water, whilst another Plate is being coated with Collodion, and placed in the Bath. The Washing Tray is now

---

* If the concave part *r* is slightly wetted with water, the adhesion to the plate is more perfect.

shaken from side to side, so as to cause the water to flow over the plate with some violence for half a minute. The water is then drained off, and its place supplied with a second and a third quantity, repeating the shaking between each addition, so as to remove *as much as possible of the Bath Solution* from the surface. The back of the Plate is finally well washed with water, and it is then placed nearly upright on filtering paper, with the face against a wall, for *one minute*, to drain; and it is then ready to receive the Albumen coating.

COATING WITH ALBUMEN.

When the Glass Plate has been allowed to drain one minute, the Plate-holder is again attached as before described, and a little of the Iodized Albumen is poured on at the upper edge, and the Plate inclined so as to cause it to flow over the entire surface, and run off into the sink. A second quantity of the Iodized Albumen is then poured over the surface so as to cover every part; then drained off, *and again poured on and off three times;* ultimately, drain off as much as possible of the excess of the Iodized Albumen, and place the Plate nearly upright against the wall, with the coated side inwards, to become surface dry; lastly, hold the Plate in front of a good fire till it is quite dry and hot. The Iodized Albumen must be filtered just prior to being used; one ounce will coat ten Plates, and what remains should be thrown away, as it will have become too diluted to be effective.

In coating with Albumen, the presence of air-bubbles or dust must be guarded against. The former can easily be done by taking care, in pouring the Albumen into the measure and on the Plate, not to pour so as to generate air-bubbles in the liquid. But should any be detected, hold the Plate horizontally, and give it another coating of Albumen, then incline the Plate so that the bulk of the liquid shall pass over and carry off the bubbles with the running stream. Dust on the Plate must be prevented by operating in a room as free from this photographic enemy as possible.

In order to render the coating of Albumen as uniform as possible, the Plate must stand to dry on two or three layers of Filtering Paper, and the upper surface must touch the wall at *one point only*, and not be allowed to rest against it along its entire upper edge.

When the Albumen coating has been thus thoroughly dried and cold, the Plate is ready to be excited; but if more have been prepared than are likely to be used for taking pictures on during the next week or ten days, they may be stowed away in a Plate-box, ready to receive the sensitive coating at any time, as these Albumenized Plates, if kept dry, will remain good for months and are not injured by light.

EXCITING THE PLATE.

Prior to the Plates being excited, they must be freed from any particles of loose dust on the surface, back, or edge. Lay the Plate, Albumen side upwards, on a glass Dipper, and plunge it with *one downward movement* into the Dipping-bath (Fig. 9), previously filled to within an inch of the top with Aceto-Nitrate Bath Solution, made as described page 16, and carefully filtered *each time* before using; allow the Plate to remain in the Bath for one minute, then raise and depress it two or three times, and then remove it. The superfluous liquid on its surface is allowed to drain back into the Bath, and the Plate is then placed in the Washing-tray, Fig. 14, (Albumen side uppermost), and well washed for at least one minute, using a continuous stream of water and agitating the Tray constantly so as to *thoroughly remove* every particle of the Bath Solution. When the Plate is thoroughly washed, it is leaned against the wall of the room to dry. The Plate having been allowed to dry (which takes place in about half an hour), it is ready for immediate exposure in the Camera, or may be stowed away in a Plate-box, and kept a week before being exposed; and it is a fact worthy of note, that Plates that have been sensitized a week are equally as sensitive as those just excited.

EXPOSURE IN THE CAMERA.

The time of exposure in the Camera varies according to the intensity of the light, and the aperture and focal length of the Lens; therefore, to give the exact time would be impossible; but as some little guide it may be mentioned, that with a Horne and Thornthwaite's Stereoscopic Lens of 4½ in. focus and ⅜ in. aperture, about one minute and a half will be required for each picture in the full sunshine of summer, three minutes in the sunshine of winter; about three minutes in the summer without sunshine, and ten minutes in winter: *but at all times expose for the deepest shades, as the high lights are but little liable to injury from over-exposure.* Speaking on this subject Mr. Sidebottom says:—

"The time of exposure is a matter in which every one must judge for himself, according to the subject, lens, aperture, light, time of year, &c. It is well in all cases to expose sufficiently long, as an over-exposed picture can be made good, but an under-exposed one cannot. There ought to be very few touches, either of pure white or black, in a good photograph. An under-exposed picture gives plenty of both."

DEVELOPING THE IMAGE.

The Plate, on being taken into the operating room, is placed on a levelling stand, and distilled or filtered rain-water poured over it for half a minute, so as completely to moisten the surface and remove any particles of adherent dust; then drain slightly, and pour over its surface a mixture made by adding six drops of Silver Developing Solution to three drams of Pyrogallic Acid Solution (made and filtered as before described). *Pour on and off repeatedly so as thoroughly to moisten every part of the Plate*, then allow it to remain on the Plate until the general outline of the picture appears. This generally occupies about one minute, although sometimes much longer. Now pour off the Developing Solution, and examine the Plate to ascertain if any stains are apparent; should such be visible, they may be easily removed *at this stage* by carefully brushing the surface with a Camel's-hair brush. When this is effected, again pour on the Developing Solution, until the picture is fully brought out in all its details, but possibly still faint. To give intensity, mix a fresh quantity of the Pyrogallic Acid Solution, with double the quantity of Silver Developing Solution first employed and pour this on and off until the desired effect is obtained. This being accomplished, drain off and thoroughly wash with water. The picture is now ready for the next operation—fixing the image.

Should the Developing fluid become muddy, pour it off, well wash the Plate, and continue the development with fresh solutions made as before.

In general a good picture takes from five minutes to half an hour to develop,* and the condition of the sky will serve to indicate whether the proper amount of exposure has been given. An under-exposed picture has a dense sky, but the details in the deep shades are deficient; whereas in an over-exposed picture the details are well out, but the sky is transparent and generally of a reddish tint ; such pictures, moreover, possess no contrasts of light and shade ; whereas when the proper amount of exposure has been given, the sky is perfectly opaque, the middle tints finely developed, and the details apparent in the deepest shades with perfect contrasts of light and shade.

Mr. Woodward, of Nottingham, who is an authority, says:— "I may as well add, that my experience has taught me the true secret in the production of good negatives, viz.— *development;* many a Plate is spoilt in this part of the manipulation by the too free use of Pyrogallic,† and *above*

---

* If the temperature of the operating room is allowed to fall below 60°, the development proceeds more slowly, or even ceases altogether. In such cases heat the Developing Solution to about 70°, and renew every five minutes until the picture is developed.

† This gentleman uses a Pyrogallic Solution made by dissolving 3 grains of Pyrogallic Acid in 3 ounces of distilled water, and adding 1 dram of Glacial Acetic Acid in hot weather, and half a dram in cold.

all, of Silver.   Amateurs generally (of course beginners) are
too impatient to see their picture; if it does not appear in
two or three minutes, more and more Silver is added, to the
utter destruction of the negative.   I am well content if my
Plate is fully developed in half or three quarters of an hour.
Pictures, with a bright sun, are of course developed in less
time; most patience is required with those exposed in dull
light."

FIXING THE IMAGE.

The Plate, having been thoroughly freed from the Developing fluid by washing, is placed on the Levelling Stand, and the
surface covered with Fixing Solution.   In a minute or two the
yellow opalescent colour of the film will disappear; and when
this occurs, well wash with water, and lean the Plate against
the wall to drain and dry.   The surface, when dry, is sufficiently
hard to resist any *slight* violence; but as a further protection,
warm the Plate all over slightly near a good fire, then pour
over its surface Horne and Thornthwaite's Negative Varnish
in the same manner as Collodion is applied.   Allow the
superfluous Varnish to drain back into the bottle; hold the
Plate again before the fire until the whole of the spirit is
evaporated, and, when cold, the Plate is ready to be printed
from, so as to produce any number of positive pictures, either
on paper or glass, as hereafter described.

A negative picture may sometimes require to be "touched,"
in order to give an increased opacity to the sky; this may be
easily done with Indian Ink, ground on a plate with water to
which a few drops of Albumen have been added.

FOTHERGILL'S PROCESS.

The Solutions for this process are :—
>Plate Cleaning Solution.
>Iodized Collodion.
>Bath Solution.
>Prepared Albumen.
>Chloride of Ammonium Solution.
>Pyrogallic Acid Solution.
>Silver Developing Solution.
>Fixing Solution.

PLATE CLEANING SOLUTION.

This is supplied by Horne and Thornthwaite in four ounce bottles, price sixpence each.

IODIZED COLLODION.

Powell's Collodion, devised for his dry process, is also found eminently successful for Fothergill's; and answers best after being iodized two or three days, and continues in full activity for months. To iodize it, add two drams of Powell's Iodizing Solution to six drams of his Collodion, shake well together, and then allow the bottle to remain undisturbed for an hour or two, then pour off the clear portion into a perfectly clean and dry bottle for use.

In operating with this volatile article or with Ether, never approach with a light near an open bottle, or accidents may arise from its inflammable nature.

BATH SOLUTION.

This solution is prepared exactly as described at page 16 for the Collodio-albumen process.

PREPARED ALBUMEN.

Take three eggs, carefully separate the yolk and germ; pour the white into a measure, which will give about 18 drams of Albumen. Add to this one ounce of water and twenty drops of Liquor Ammonia; stir the whole together with a glass rod for two minutes, and leave it to rest for about twelve hours. Then strain through fine muslin, and store away in a bottle for use.

Albumen, thus prepared, will keep good a considerable time, but must be diluted with an equal bulk of Chloride of Ammonium Solution described below, and filtered through sponge, just prior to being poured on the Plate. Decomposition shows itself by the fluid becoming opaque, and with stringy masses floating with it. When this occurs reject it at once, and prepare a fresh quantity.

CHLORIDE OF AMMONIUM SOLUTION.

Chloride of Ammonium - - 2 scruples.
Distilled or Filtered Rain Water 4 ounces.

Dissolve and filter.

PYROGALLIC SOLUTION.

Pyrogallic Acid - - - - 8 grains.
Citric Acid - - - - 2 grains.
Distilled or Filtered Rain Water - 4 ounces.

Dissolve and Filter.

This solution will not keep good more than a few days in summer.

The above strength of Developing Solution is to be employed when the operating room is about 60° F.; but the quantity of Pyrogallic Acid must be diminished in summer and increased in winter.

SILVER DEVELOPING SOLUTION.

Nitrate of Silver - - - - 20 grains.
Distilled or Filtered Rain Water - 1 ounce.
Dissolve and Filter.

FIXING SOLUTION.

Hyposulphite of Soda - - - 4 ounces.
Water - - - - - 16 ounces.
Dissolve.

The Glass Plate is made thoroughly clean and coated with Collodion,* as described at page 19, and the film is allowed to set until the drop at the lowest corner loses its fluidity, and is capable of being impressed by the finger. When this takes place it is immersed in the Bath Solution as there described; and allowed to remain one minute: it is then lifted out two or three times, in order to facilitate the removal of the *oily appearance* which the Plate now presents. When the surface appears uniformly wetted, the plate is removed from the Dipper, and the excess of solution drained off. It is then placed, Collodion-side-upwards, in a gutta percha tray, as described at page 12, into which (for a stereoscopic size plate) six drams of water has been introduced. The tray is then gently inclined, so that the water may flow over *every part* of the Plate, in all directions: continue this for about half a minute, or until the greasy appearance caused by the water coming in contact with the Plate is entirely removed.

Then remove the Plate by a silver hook, attach the Globe plate-holder, and bring it horizontal; and pour over its surface Dilute Albumen, made as follows:—Take of the prepared Albumen, and Chloride of Ammonium Solution, made as before described, of each half an ounce, stir together with a clean glass rod, and filter through a fragment of sponge, slightly plugged into the neck of a clean glass funnel.

* This, and all other operations (except exposure in the camera), must take place in a room from which white light is carefully excluded; as described at page 18.

Pour (for a stereoscopic plate) one dram of this Dilute Albumen over the surface, so as to cover every part; drain off and again pour on and off four or five times slowly, so that the Albumen may be in contact with the Plate *at least* half a minute; ultimately, drain off as much as possible of the excess of the Albumen, and place the Plate, face upwards, in a Washing-tray, made as Fig. 14, previously filled with water; shake the tray from side to side with some violence, so as to agitate the water thoroughly for ten seconds: drain off the water and again fill the tray by pouring fresh water into it, so as to fall at the part *a* of the tray, and *not on the surface of the film*. Again agitate for ten seconds, throw out the second water, fill up and agitate again for another ten seconds; then lift the plate out with a silver hook, and stand up to drain until surface dry, in a cupboard, perfectly free from light, with one corner resting on two or three thicknesses of filtering paper; so that the upper surface may touch the wall at *one point only;* lastly, complete the drying in an oven, or by artificial means, taking care that the temperature does not exceed 130°.

When these Plates are thoroughly dry, they may be placed in the Camera-backs, or stowed away in light-tight boxes, and carefully protected from chemical or sulphurous vapours; and, as far as can at present be judged, they will keep an indefinite time, *as not the slightest deterioration or loss of sensibility has occurred in plates kept three months in summer.*

It is found most advisable to reject the Albumen after being once used, and to coat the next Plate with another quantity, also to reject the water after being used to wash one plate in the first tray, and to take a fresh quantity for the next plate.

In coating with Albumen, the presence of air-bubbles or dust must be guarded against. The former can easily be done by taking care, in pouring the Albumen into the measure, and on the Plate, not to pour so as to generate air-bubbles in the liquid. But should any be detected, hold the plate horizontally, and give it another coating of Albumen, then incline the Plate so that the bulk of the liquid shall pass over and carry off the bubbles with the running stream. Dust on the plate must be prevented by operating in a room as free from this photographic enemy as possible.

EXPOSURE IN THE CAMERA.

The time of exposure in the Camera varies according to the intensity of the light, and the aperture and focal length of the Lens; therefore to give the exact time would be impossible, but, as a general rule, a light building, well illuminated by sunlight, would require about :—

40 seconds with Lens of $4\frac{1}{4}$ in. focus, and $\frac{1}{4}$ in. stop.

1 minute	„	$5\frac{1}{4}$	„	$\frac{1}{4}$
$1\frac{1}{2}$ „	„	10	„	$\frac{1}{2}$
3 „	„	14	„	$\frac{1}{2}$
4 „	„	16	„	$\frac{1}{2}$

A light building with foliage requires about one-fourth longer exposure; but for masses of rock, and foliage of a dark character, three or four times the exposure above stated. In winter, all these exposures must be doubled; *but at all times expose for the deepest shades, as the high lights are but little liable to injury from over-exposure.*

DEVELOPING THE IMAGE.

The plate, on being taken into the operating room, is placed on a levelling stand, and distilled or filtered rain-water poured over it for half a minute, so as completely to moisten every part of the surface and remove any particles of adherent dust; then drain slightly, and pour over its surface a mixture of (for a stereoscopic plate) six drops of Silver Developing Solution, and four drams of Pyrogallic Solution. Pour this on and off repeatedly, from opposite corners, so as to keep it constantly on the move.

The image appears rapidly;*but should the developing solution become turbid, throw it away, and mix a second quantity, and if the development appears unequal, wash the plate with water, drain slightly, and pour on newly-mixed developing fluid repeatedly, to the weakest part, until an equalisation is effected; then cover the whole surface, and continue pouring on and off until the image is sufficiently intense. Lastly, wash so as to free the surface from the developing fluid, and the picture is ready for fixing.

In general a good picture takes from two to four minutes to develope, and the indications of an under or over exposed negative are precisely similar to those described at page 25.

FIXING THE IMAGE.

The Plate having been thoroughly freed from the developing fluid by washing, is fixed and varnished in the same manner as described at page 26, and is then ready to be printed from, so as to produce any number of positive pictures, on either paper or glass.

CONCLUDING HINTS.

Clean the Glass Plates carefully with very clean cloths, avoiding especially those used to wipe the hands after coating with Albumen.

Filter the Bath Solution whenever about to prepare a lot of Plates; and, when not in use, keep it in a stoppered bottle, in a dark corner of the operating room, so that the full glare of daylight may at no time fall on it.

Allow the collodion to set thoroughly before immersion in

---

* If the temperature of the operating room is allowed to fall below 60°, the development proceeds more slowly, or even ceases altogether. In such cases heat the developing solution to about 80°, and renew as often as necessary.

the Nitrate Bath, or it may become detached in washing or after fixing; but, as a matter of course, this must not be carried so far that any part may become dry, or the Nitrate Bath will act unequally on the film.

Iodized Collodion that has become too thick for use by evaporation may be diluted with rectified Sulphuric Ether; but *Methylated* Ether must not be used for this purpose.

After sensitising the Collodion film, wash as described, and do not allow water to fall directly on the surface of the Plate, or unequal patches will show themselves in developing.

The Dilute Albumen that has been employed to coat one Plate must be thrown away, and a second quantity taken for the next Plate.

Use two globe Plate-holders, one for collodionising the Plate, and the second for coating with Albumen; but carefully avoid using the one ordinarily employed for the Albumen to coat a Plate with Collodion, as Albumen would thus be introduced into the Bath Solution, which would speedily spoil it for the purpose.

Handle the coated Plate as little as possible, and always wash the hands after coating with Albumen before removing another Plate from the Bath; indeed, never take up a Plate without washing and drying the hands on a clean towel.

Give a full exposure in the Camera, or the resulting negative will be harsh, and produce black and white prints without middle tints.

Keep the glass used for the Developing Mixture perfectly clean.

Take especial care that no gleam of white light falls on the Plates during preparation or drying, and when dry, stow away in *light-tight* boxes of mahogany or tin, if not required for immediate use.

In developing take especial care that the Developing Fluid is kept on the move by being repeatedly poured on and off the Plate, or mottling will be the result.

D

Guard against over development, as a comparatively weak negative by this process will print well, owing to the nature of the deposit forming the shades having a greater action in stopping the light whilst printing than that produced by the ordinary Collodion process.

POWELL'S NEW DRY PROCESS.

Without entering into particulars or drawing comparisons between the rival *dry* processes of which tribe there is a legion, we now proceed to give the one invented by Mr. John Harrison Powell; leaving the reader to decide as to its merits : but, in doing so, I must say that since it was communicated to me by the inventor (in January last), I have used no other, and the results obtained are superior to any of my former productions, and can vie for excellence with those produced by any other process; whilst in pourtraying *distance*, I consider this process superior to *any other* (either wet or dry), whilst the certainty of success is very great.

THE SOLUTIONS NECESSARY

For this process are—

> Plate Cleaning Solution.
> Iodized Collodion.
> Bath Solution.
> Preservative Solution.
> Pyrogallic Solution.
> Silver Developing Solution.
> Fixing Solution.

PLATE CLEANING SOLUTION.

This can be obtained ready for use of Messrs. Horne and Thornthwaite in four ounce bottles, at sixpence each.

IODIZED COLLODION.

Iodized Collodion to be suitable for this process must yield a creamy film when excited, possess great sensibility, and be of a contractile nature; and as such a Collodion was not to be met with, Mr. Powell turned his attention to this important point, and has succeeded in producing a Collodion suitable for any dry process, and equally available for the wet process. To iodize it for his new process—mix two drams of the Iodizing Compound with six drams of the Collodion, and after allowing it to stand twelve hours, pour off the clear portion into a clean and dry bottle, and it is fit for immediate use, and must not be employed *for this process* if it has been iodized longer than a month. This limitation arises from a *mechanical* change which appears to take place in the condition of the film; as its sensibility remains unimpaired for three months after being iodized.

BATH SOLUTION.

The Bath Solution for this process is prepared as described at page 16. A weaker Bath is often the cause of failures, and must not be employed.

The proper condition is *slightly* acid, and Test Paper should be frequently employed to ascertain if it is in this condition. "Clark's" Test Paper answers best for this purpose. A drop of the solution applied to a leaf of this paper should change the colour to a pale red. If no change of colour, or an increase of blueness is produced, a drop, or even two, of Glacial Acetic Acid must be added to each pint of Bath Solution : or should the Test Paper change at once to a bright red, the Bath contains too much acid, and a fragment of the size of a pin's head of Carbonate of Soda may be expected to restore it to its normal condition.

The Bath Solution should be tested by the Bath Tester, page 48, after coating about three dozen Plates to ascertain if the quantity of Nitrate of Silver to each ounce of water has varied, as, if such is the case, more Nitrate of Silver must be added to restore it to its original strength.

PRESERVATIVE SOLUTION.

Glycyrrhizine Solution   -   -   1 ounce.
Distilled or Filtered Rain Water - 4 ounces.

Mix, and filter prior to using.

Much of the delay in publishing this process arose from a desire to supply Glycyrrhizine in a solid state; but, after experiments for months, this was found totally impracticable, as this peculiar substance changes its condition in drying to such an extent as often to be utterly useless when again dissolved. To remedy this defect, Glycyrrhizine will be supplied in solution only, in 4-ounce bottles, price 2s. 6d.

The Pyrogallic Solution, Silver Developing and Fixing Solutions, are made as described at pages 28 & 29.

The Plate is cleaned, coated with the above Iodized Collodion, and placed in the Bath Solution as described at pages 19 and 20, where it is allowed to remain two minutes; it is then lifted out two or three times, in order to facilitate the removal of the *oily appearance* which the Plate now presents. When the surface appears uniformly wetted, the Plate is removed from the Dipper, and the excess of solution drained off; it is then placed, Collodion-side upwards, in a Washing Tray made as fig. 14, in which has been previously placed about six ounces of water (ordinary water, if not too hard, will answer); incline the Tray so that the water may flow gently over the surface of the Plate in all directions for about twenty times; then pour off and add another six ounces of water, cause this to flow over the Plate about ten or a dozen times; then pour off the water; drain for a second only; and then apply the Preservative Solution.

To do this, attach the globe Plate-holder, bring the Plate horizontal, and pour on at one end one dram of the Preservative Solution (carefully filtered), and incline the Plate so that it may flow over the entire surface and run off into the sink.   Drain for about a quarter of a minute; and pour a second dram of the Preservative Solution on and off, *slowly*, six or seven times, so as to occupy *at least* one minute; then drain and place to dry in a perfectly dark box or cupboard, with one corner resting on two or three thicknesses of Filtering Paper, so that the upper surface may touch the wall at *one point only*.

The film of these Plates is *sometimes* liable to become loose and slip off *after fixing*, unless some method is now adopted to prevent it. To avoid this, take a camel's hair pencil, the size of the drawing, and tie a slip of wood to it as there represented, so that the wood may project about a quarter of an inch below the brush. Dip this prepared brush into Horne and Thornthwaite's Negative Varnish; and holding it upright, and using the projecting slip of wood as a guide, carry it round the four edges of the Plate, so as to leave a film of Varnish about one-eighth of an inch wide all round.*

Fig. 15.

This Varnish will dry in five minutes, and the plates may then be placed in the Camera-backs, or stowed away in light-tight boxes. If carefully protected from damp, chemical or sulphurous vapours, and in a cool place, they will retain their sensitiveness for months, even in summer.

The Preservative Solution used to finish one Plate after being carefully filtered may be used as the first coating for a second Plate.

EXPOSURE.

The exposure in the Camera is about the same as given for Fothergill's Plates, page 31. It is absolutely essential to give long exposures with this or any other dry process in order to obtain soft pictures with good half tones, more especially with objects having great contrast of light and shade.

* This brush requires to be kept in a separate bottle containing a little Alcohol, in order to prevent the varnish on it becoming hard and dry, and thus rendering it unfit for use.

DEVELOPMENT, FIXING, AND VARNISHING.

The Plate is developed, fixed, and varnished as described at page 31, using the developing fluids mentioned at pages 28 and 29. The operation of development takes about two minutes; but, if from imperfect light, the time is prolonged, the operator must have patience, and not use an excess of the Silver Developing Solution, which, although it may hasten the development, will certainly spoil the beauty of the result.

Should the sky not be sufficiently dense before the details in the deep shades are well out, it may be intensified by using a developing mixture, containing twice the quantity of Silver Developing Solution first used.

OPERATIONS FOR TAKING A STEREOSCOPIC PICTURE.

Having prepared a number of sensitive plates by either one or other of the three processes before given, we will suppose the operator has obtained one of Powell's Cameras, and desires to use it forthwith. The first operation necessarily is to transfer the sensitive Plates to the double backs. To do this the Camera must be taken into the operating room, and the door closed so as to exclude all white light. One of the Camera-backs is taken and opened as shewn in Fig. 16, and

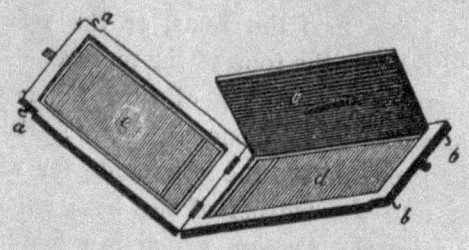

Fig. 16.

an excited Plate laid Collodion-side downwards in the side *d*, or next the sliding flap, and the hinged flap *c* closed down and secured by the turnbuckle; and a second Plate is then placed face downwards in the part *e*, and the back is then closed, and prevented from again opening by the hook *a a;* the sliding flaps are also secured by the hooks *b b.*

In exactly the same manner, two excited Plates can be placed in each Camera-back, and when all are filled, they are put into their respective grooves in the box. The whole is examined to see everything is in its place; the door is locked and the legs of the stand are buckled together; and all is ready for a trip which may take hours or days.

On arriving near any object we desire to portray, the View-meter (Fig. 5) is first employed, so as to determine on what spot the Camera must be fixed in order to obtain the most artistic picture. This is easily done by holding the ring of this little instrument between the finger and thumb of the right hand, so that the smallest aperture is close to the eye. Exactly as much of the view as is visible when looking through the instrument would be taken by the Camera if placed on the same spot,* and the operator must then judge by trial, whether by advancing or receding a more artistic picture would be produced. As it is to be borne in mind, in taking photographs, that it is not sufficient to fix up a Camera on any casual spot to ensure a good picture; something more must be done in selecting the proper situation to obtain the best effect of light and shade.

In taking any object, the Camera must be so placed that the sun shall not shine into the Lens, or the reflection caused thereby would destroy the tone of the picture.

Having selected the best point of view, the next step is to set up the Camera. This is done as follows:—Screw it on the stand with the lock towards the left hand; for which purpose a plate is let into the bottom of the box; unlock, and turn back the lid; raise the Camera, which is a folding one; press the front into its position (the Lens being already on it); turn the Camera at right angles, with the Lens pointing towards the object to be taken; open the door at the end of the box; take out the Back-holder and Focusing Glass, and place them in the groove at the back of the Camera made to receive them, being careful that a mark on the Focussing Glass is opposite a corresponding one on the Back-holder. The apparatus will then be as represented in the Fig. 17.

The Camera slides on a grove, which is continued along the top of the box and the inside of the lid. By this means a movement of any length up to 13 inches can be obtained, and can be varied according to the distance of the object from the Lens. A scale of inches is engraved on the edge of the

---

* This is supposing the Lens having the shortest focus is to be used.

groove, to determine the length of movement of the Camera between taking the first and second picture.

Fig 17.

A portion of the groove is also made moveable at the left-hand side by a screw, in order to adjust the angle. The brass mounting is constructed to take two Lenses of different foci, the one not in use fitting on to the door of the box.

To arrange the apparatus for taking a picture:—Slide the Camera to the right until its right-hand edge rests on the line registering the number of inches of movement required to be used. This distance must be determined by the proximity of the nearest prominent object in the foreground of the proposed picture. If this distance is only a few feet, three inches of movement will suffice; if twenty feet, five or six inches may be used; and in taking a panoramic view, or where nothing of importance occurs in the foreground, within fifty yards, the whole length of movement will give the most stereoscopic results.

The next object to be determined will be which Lens to employ—the long or short focus one. The short focus one will be found the one most generally used for buildings, interiors, &c.; but for portraying near and DISTANT objects combined in one picture, the long focus Lens will be the most useful, and in nearly every case is to be preferred for panoramic views.

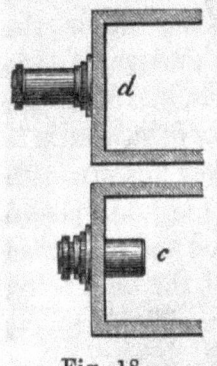

It will be noticed that the outer or Jacket tube of the Lens furnished with Powell's Camera has a double screw, and can be screwed into the Camera so as to project *inwards*, as at *c*, Fig. 18, (where the Camera is shewn in section); or by being reversed to project *outward*, as at *d*, Fig. 18. It is therefore necessary, when changing the short for the long focus Lens, to withdraw the tube *b*, Fig. 19,

Fig 18.

unscrew the short focus Lens, and screw the long focus Lens into the same tube; the Jacket *c*, Fig. 18, is then to be unscrewed, reversed, and again screwed in so as to project as at *d*; lastly, the tube *b*, containing the Lens, is pushed into the Jacket.

Fig 19.

Changing from the long to the short focus is but a reversal of the foregoing; but the Jacket must in this case be screwed in as at *c*. Always withdraw the tube *b* before making a change of Lenses, and do not replace it until the Jacket is screwed on to the Camera in the required position.

All this being done the apparatus is ready for focussing; but, prior to doing so, the Circular Level on the top of the Camera, must be noticed to ascertain if it has been set perfectly level. This is at once apparent, for if such is the case, the spirit-bubble will be in the centre of the level; and if it is not so, one or other of the stand-legs must be shifted until the desired position is obtained.

Focussing requires some care, and should be practised frequently before attempting to take a view at a distance from home. To do this, fix the Camera on the Camera-stand, with the Lens pointed to some prominent object, as in Fig. 17, and remove the Lens-cap, placing the focussing screen in its place, as shown in the figure. Draw up the flap in front of the Focussing Glass, and an inverted picture of all objects in front of the Camera will be visible on the ground glass. In order to render this picture as sharp and perfect as possible, throw the Focussing Cloth over the head and back of the Camera, so as to shut out all light except what enters the Lens, and slide the Lens forward or back, until the greatest amount of sharpness is produced; but as the unassisted eye can scarcely discern with sufficient exactness, the Focussing Eye-piece (Fig. 4) is placed with its narrow end on the ground glass, and the magnified picture inspected by looking into the other end, the Lens being shifted as before described, until the greatest possible sharpness of the picture is produced.

Should there appear too much foreground in the picture, loosen the screw in front of the Camera, and raise the slide which carries the Lens; and if there is too much sky, depress it, *but in no case should the Camera be either elevated or depressed to effect the same object.* Having focussed with great care, observe what part of some prominent object in the picture bisects the vertical pencil line on the Focussing Screen, then move the Camera to the left, as far as the groove will allow it to go, and notice whether the same part of the object now occupies the same position as before; should a difference be noticed, turn the screw which adjusts the moveable part of the groove either to the right or left until the error observed is rectified; and if this is properly done, shifting the Camera from side to side will not change the position of the picture on the ground glass. The flap having been shut down, and the Focussing Screen removed, the first back with the sliding flap, marked No. 1, is pushed into its place, having previously opened the fastening at *b* Fig. 16, so that the flap No. 1, *is inside,* and the mark on the Back-holder shall be opposite to a corresponding mark on the back. The Camera is now drawn to the *right-hand side*, so that it occupies the same position as in focussing; the flap is drawn up, and the Lens-cap removed for the necessary time of exposure for the light to produce the required impression on the Plate. When the required time has been given, the Lens-cap is replaced, the back is pushed inwards to the fullest extent into the back-holder, the Camera is shifted to the *left-hand side* of the box, as far as it can be moved, and the Lens-cap is again removed for the same amount of time* as in taking the first picture.

When this time has elapsed, replace the Lens-cap, shut down the flap, and remove the back from the Camera; but in doing so, push in the sliding shutter with the right hand, as the left hand removes it from the Camera, or a gleam of light will fall on the Plate and spoil your picture. The fastening *b* is now closed, and the second Plate may be exposed to the same object in exactly the same manner, or retained until we arrive at some other object considered worthy of being pourtrayed, by merely reversing the double back, so that flap No. 2, is this time *inside*. In this way we may proceed until the eight Plates have been impressed. On reaching home, the next operation will be the developement of the pictures, as before described; but this may be deferred for some days, if required, thus enabling us to take even a distant tour with Plates prepared before leaving home: expose them during the journey, and leave the development until our return.

DOUBLE LENS STEREOSCOPIC CAMERAS.

It will be noticed that with the foregoing Cameras the views are taken consecutively, and that they are specially intended for architectural subjects, buildings, panoramas, still life, &c., where there are no moving figures. When there is a proba-

---

* This is supposing the light remains the same during the two exposures. If any variation should take place, a longer time must be given to the picture taken in the dullest light.

bility of the figures moving, as in taking portraits, landscapes with cattle, &c., the Binocular Camera must be employed.

These are of two kinds, the first intended for portraits, and the second for views.

A Binocular Camera for portraits consists of a pair of portrait Lenses of equal foci affixed to an expanding Camera. This is usually supplied with Focussing Glass and one back only, and is intended for taking portraits and groups by the "wet" process.

The second form of Binocular Camera is represented by fig. 20. This is another form of Powell's registered Camera, and is

Fig. 20.

constructed on nearly the same principles, and is of about the same size and weight. The description given for using Powell's Single Lens Camera is so nearly what would apply for this form that it is scarcely necessary to repeat it ; the main difference being that the sliding flap of the back-holder is pulled entirely out at once, and that both Lenses must be uncovered and re-covered at the same time. In some cases where rapidity is no object, it may be necessary to give a greater degree of stereoscopic effect than can be produced by this Camera when used to take both pictures simultaneously. To do this, having focussed and inserted the Camera-back with its Sensitive Plate, we slide the Camera to the left hand side of the box, and uncover the left hand Lens for the required time, then cover this, slide the Camera to the right the required distance, and then uncover the right hand Lens as long as necessary. By doing this we can by a Binocular Camera produce an extra amount of stereoscopic effect, but negatives taken by either fig. 20 or the Binocular Portrait Camera cannot be conveniently used to print glass transparent positives, as the resulting pictures require to be cut, and the pictures transposed before they can be viewed stereoscopically. For this reason, and also for the stereoscopic effect being more pleasing, the author has lately discarded the Binocular Camera, and now uses one of Powell's Cameras, fig. 7, for taking stereoscopic views.

THE PRINTING PROCESS.

Before entering into the details of the next operation, it is necessary that the amateur should possess a clear idea of the meaning of the terms "positive" and "negative."

A positive picture may be defined to be a photograph giving a natural representation of the object it is intended to represent when viewed by reflected or transmitted light.

A negative picture, on the contrary, when viewed by reflected light, gives but an imperfect representation of the object from which it was taken, having the high lights of the picture obscure and of a brown colour, without any apparent definition of middle tints, or the lights and shades merging into one another with abruptness; but if viewed by transmitted light, the lights and shades are reversed—representing all the pure whites of the object by perfect blackness, the blacks by perfect transparency, and the middle tints of various gradations of tone in the same *inverse* order, according as the parts represented are more or less approaching the white or sombre shades.

A good negative, prepared as before described, may be used to produce an infinite number of positives, and the process for their production is termed "printing." These positives may either be on paper or glass; the former is viewed by reflected, and the latter by transmitted light.

As in former editions, I propose to refer those who desire to reproduce positives on paper to "Thornthwaite's Guide to Photography" for full particulars, first mentioning that good positive pictures on glass are by far the most pleasing, are easier of production, and admit of finer detail. They are also *more permanent* than those on paper. Another recommendation is, that glass positives may be as successfully printed by artificial as by day light, and require no extra solutions; the addition of a pressure frame to the articles used for negatives being all that is necessary.

TO PRODUCE GLASS POSITIVES.

The Pressure Frame for printing glass positives consists of a wooden frame of the same internal measurement as the glass we employ for our negatives, and is furnished with a projected rim on which the negative may rest. A Back-board, lined with cloth, also fits into the frame, which firmly presses the prepared Plate against the negative when the cross-bars are fastened down by their respective hooks.

To produce glass positives, close the door of the operating room, place the negative, *face upwards*, in the pressure frame, and on it, *face downwards*, lay a Sensitive Plate, prepared by Powell's process; the Back-board is then laid on the Sensitive Plate, and the cross-bars fastened down, so as to bring the sensitive coating on the plate in direct contact with the negative; wrap up the Pressure Frame in the Focussing Cloth, open the door of the operating room, and all is ready for exposure. The direct rays of the sun are far too energetic for our purpose, therefore remove the Focussing Cloth, and expose the frame, face upwards, to the northern part of the sky, from two to five seconds, according to the intensity of the light; then again cover up with the Focussing Cloth, return to the operating room, close the door, and proceed to develop and fix the image, as described at page 31*. If the operator cannot conveniently make use of daylight for printing, place the pressure frame in front of, and six inches from, an argand oil lamp or gaslight, and allow it to remain undisturbed about two minutes; then proceed to the development as before described. When these pictures are developed, fixed, and thoroughly dry, they may be mounted ready for viewing by the stereoscope in Stereoscopic passe-partouts made for the purpose.

BATH TESTER.

In working with either the wet or dry process, it is absolutely essential that the Bath Solution should be preserved as near as possible to its original strength; and if it falls much below this strength, Nitrate of Silver must be added to supply the deficiency.

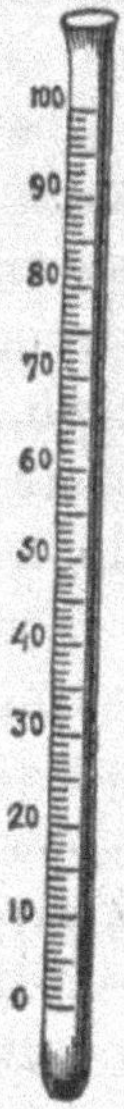

Many instruments have been devised for this purpose, but the form shown by Fig. 21 is the most simple in action, and sufficiently exact for the purpose. To use it we must proceed as follows:—

Take of highly dried and perfectly pure Chloride of Sodium $84\frac{1}{4}$ grains, and dissolve it in 20 ounces of distilled water. This forms the Test Solution, and requires to be made with exactness, or the result obtained by its use will be erroneous. A second solution is also needed; this is made by dissolving 20 grains of Bichromate of Potash in 1 ounce of water.

To test the strength of a Bath Solution, take the Bath Tester, Fig. 21, and drop into it ONE DROP *only* of Bichromate of Potash Solution, then fill the tube up to the lowest division marked 0 with the Bath Solution, and add the standard Test Solution gradually, shaking at

Fig. 21

* The Pyrogallic and Silver Developing Solutions, described at pages 28 and 29, must be employed.

frequent intervals; when the colour of the precipitate, which was at first brick red, changes to a lighter tint; add the Test Solution more gradually, and continue to shake up between each addition. Continue to add the Test Solution drop by drop until the red tint of the precipitate suddenly changes to white, showing that all the Nitrate of Silver is decomposed, and that enough Test Solution has been added. Now read off the division on the level with the surface of the fluid in the Bath Tester, and it will be equal to the number of grains of Nitrate of Silver contained in each ounce of the Bath Solution. Thus, supposing, after having performed the experiment, the fluid in the Bath Tester stood level with the 39th division (counting from below upwards, the same as the tube is figured), this would indicate that each ounce of the Bath Solution tested contained 39 grains of Nitrate of Silver.

This plan of using Bichromate of Potash to show by a change of colour when all the Nitrate of Silver is converted into Chloride was published some years since in the Photographic Journal, and although but little used, answers perfectly in all cases except to test the Aceto-nitrate of Silver bath, after having been used to excite Collodio-albumen Plates. In this case, the precipitate which forms on adding the Test Solution remains coloured, however much is added, therefore, the use of the Bichromate of Potash Solution must here be dispensed with, and the Test Solution added gradually, shaking after each addition, and allowing the white Chloride of Silver which is formed, to settle down, until the Test Solution ceases to produce any more cloudiness in the clear portion of the contents. The division level with the surface of the fluid in the Bath-tester here also indicates the number of grains of Nitrate of Silver per ounce.

Printed by W. H. COX, 5, Great Queen Street, Lincoln's Inn Fields.

.